Disney

This magical book belongs to

_____

This is the story of an adventuresome lion cub,
who must find his own place in the great Circle of Life.

As the morning sun rose high over the African plain, animals and birds gathered at the foot of Pride Rock. This was a very special day!

The animals bowed when they saw the new prince, Simba.

King Mufasa and Queen Sarabi watched as Rafiki, the wise baboon, presented their newborn son to the kingdom.

Simba grew into a playful and curious cub. Early one morning, Mufasa brought Simba to the top of Pride Rock.

"Everything the light touches is our kingdom," he told his son. "One day, Simba, the sun will set on my time here, and will rise with you as the new king. We are all connected in the great Circle of Life."

Later that day, Simba went to see his Uncle Scar.

"My dad just showed me the whole kingdom," the cub bragged. "And I'm gonna rule it all!"

Now, Scar was angry that he was no longer next in line to be king. He was plotting to get rid of this new prince. He asked slyly if Mufasa had shown him what was beyond the northern border.

"Well, no," said Simba sadly. "He said I can't go there."

"And he's absolutely right," said Scar. "Far too dangerous. Only the bravest lions go there. An elephant graveyard is no place for a young prince."

Simba didn't see his uncle's evil trap. He decided to show his father what a brave cub he could be.

Simba set out to find his best friend, Nala—and go visit the elephant graveyard that very day. He had no idea that Scar had ordered three hyenas to go to the elephant graveyard, too—to kill the new prince!

Simba raced ahead across the plains, leading Nala to the forbidden place. Eventually they reached a pile of bones.

"It's really creepy," said Nala.

Simba was about to explore a skull, when he saw Zazu, his father's adviser.

Zazu commanded them to leave immediately, saying,
"You are in very real danger."

But it was already too late! Nala and Simba were
trapped by three laughing, drooling hyenas!

Simba took a deep breath and tried to roar—but only
a squeaky rumble came out. The hyenas laughed even
more at that.

Simba took another deep breath.

"*ROAARR!*"

The three hyenas looked around into the eyes of…

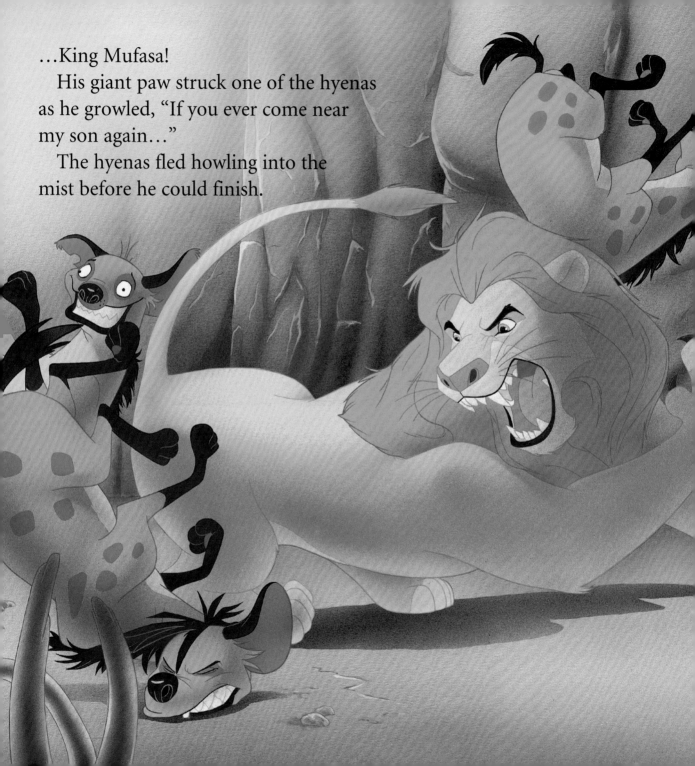

…King Mufasa!

His giant paw struck one of the hyenas as he growled, "If you ever come near my son again…"

The hyenas fled howling into the mist before he could finish.

Mufasa scolded his son on the way home. "You deliberately disobeyed me."

"I was just trying to be brave, like you," said Simba softly.

"Being brave doesn't mean you go looking for trouble," replied Mufasa.

The moon shone brightly above them and the stars twinkled in the dark sky.

Mufasa stopped. "Look at the stars! The great kings of the past look down on us from those stars. So, whenever you feel alone, just remember that those kings will always be there to guide you, and so will I."

After a long while, Simba awoke. Everything around him looked different. There were trees and grass and flowers instead of desert.

A meerkat named Timon and a warthog named Pumbaa had brought him to their home.

"You nearly died," said Pumbaa.

"I saved you!" cried Timon. "Well, uh, Pumbaa helped."

"Thanks for your help," said Simba, but he thought, *It doesn't matter. I've got nowhere to go.*

"Where ya going?" asked Timon kindly.

"Nowhere," said Simba.

"Anything we can do?" said Pumbaa.

"Not unless you can change the past," said Simba.

"You gotta put the past behind ya," said Timon. "Repeat after me: *hakuna matata!*"

"It means: no worries!" added Pumbaa.

Simba thought for a moment and decided to stay in the jungle with his new friends.

Years passed and Simba grew into a young lion. He lived a happy, carefree, no-worries life with his friends.

But one day something happened that was *not* a no-worries situation! A fierce lioness was about to spring onto Pumbaa, who was stuck under a tree root!

"She's gonna eat me!" squealed Pumbaa.

Simba rushed over to help.

Meanwhile, back at the Pride Lands, storm clouds had gathered and a lightning bolt scorched the earth. As the dry grasses caught fire, huge flames swept toward Pride Rock—and a lion appeared through the smoke.

It was Simba!

Scar lunged at Simba, determined to kill him just as he had Mufasa. Timon and Pumbaa joined in the fierce battle that followed. Simba finally heaved Scar over a cliff. Scar called to the hyenas to save him, but Simba and the lionesses drove them back.

Simba was victorious!

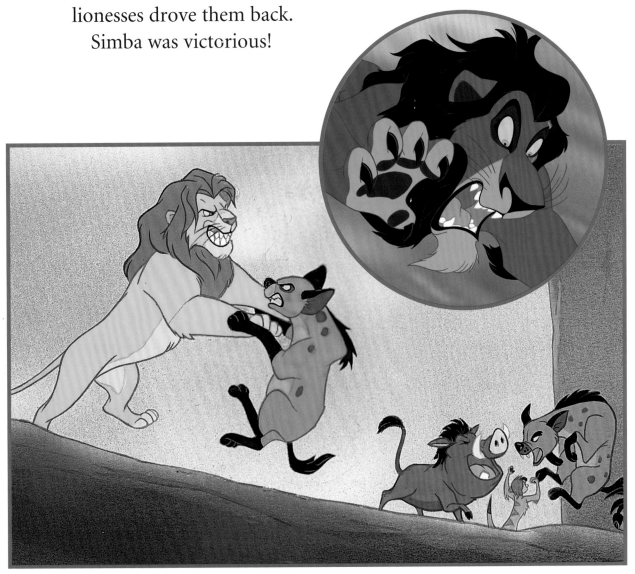

Simba took his rightful place as the Lion King, and once again the land flourished.

One dawn, the animals and birds made their way again to the foot of Pride Rock. Rafiki picked up a tiny cub. He showed the new princess—the daughter of King Simba and Queen Nala—to the cheering crowd below.

The Circle of Life would continue.